PADDINGTON'S
FINEST HOUR

PADDINGTON'S
FINEST HOUR

by MICHAEL BOND

illustrated by R.W. ALLEY

HARPER
An Imprint of HarperCollinsPublishers

Library of Congress Control Number: 2017942888
ISBN: 978-0-06-266972-8

Book design by Rick Farley
17 18 19 20 21   PC/LSCH   10 9 8 7 6 5 4 3 2 1
❖
Originally published in Great Britain by HarperCollins Children's Books in 2017
First Harper US edition, 2017

CONTENTS

Chapter One

PARKING PROBLEMS

"It's none of my business," said the police-man, "but there's an old codger in the back of your car, and he's got a sandwich on his head. Leastways, it was there a moment ago when he raised his hat—I don't know where it is now."

"He would hardly have a sandwich on *top* of his hat," said Mr. Brown, easing the driving-side window slightly shut in order to protect himself from the rain. "He isn't English, and he has his funny little ways."

"You mean he's one of them illegal immigrants?" said the policeman.

"I wouldn't call him that," said Mr. Brown cautiously. "He does have a Peruvian passport, so you could say he's here on an extended holiday. He wouldn't hurt a fly, but just to be on the safe side he keeps a marmalade sandwich under his hat in case he has an emergency."

"Heaven help him if anyone from Health and Safety catches him at it," retorted the policeman. "They're going to blow a gasket and I wouldn't blame them. I only hope it doesn't catch on."

"I've never heard of anyone else doing it," said Mr. Brown.

"And he certainly isn't an old codger," broke in Mrs. Brown.

"Pardon me, ma'am." The policeman

lowered himself until he was level with the front passenger seat. "But he could do with a good shave whatever age he is. That's all I can say."

"In that case, if you don't mind, I'll close this window," said Mr. Brown, seizing the opportunity. "I'm getting soaked."

"*You're* getting soaked!" repeated the policeman. There was a rustle of oilskin. "Wait until you're where I'm standing . . ." The rest of what he was about to say was drowned by the sound of rain beating against glass as Mr. Brown beat him to it and wound the window tightly shut.

"Was that wise, Henry?" asked Mrs. Brown. "He's getting his notebook out now."

"Good luck to him," said Mr. Brown. "Catch me getting out of the car in this weather, Mary. I haven't even got a top coat. And the chances of him writing anything in his notebook are pretty remote."

"But we *are* parked on a double yellow line," said Mrs. Brown. "On a bend."

"Along with a dozen other cars," said Mr. Brown. "Goodness knows what's going on ahead of us. There's nothing coming the other way."

Rummaging in her handbag, Mrs. Brown removed a handkerchief, and having folded it carefully into a small pad, made use of it to wipe a hole in the steamed-up windscreen. She gazed mournfully at the spot where they had come to rest.

"I don't remember it being quite so bad for a long time," she said. "It's still raining cats and dogs."

Paddington peered over her shoulder. Although he couldn't see any actual cats, or any stray dogs for that matter, he caught the general drift of the conversation and given the raindrops were literally bouncing off the pavement ahead of them like things possessed, he put two and two together and made five.

"I expect it would be worse in Darkest Peru, Mrs. Brown," he said. "They don't have any pavements there, but it might even rain cats and bears."

"Heaven forbid!" exclaimed Mr. Brown.

"Things said in jest often have a habit of turning out to be true, Henry," warned Mrs. Brown. "Are you quite sure you want to stop and post a letter? Can't it wait a day or two?"

"Unfortunately, no," said Mr. Brown. "It's the main reason why I came out in the first place."

"In that case, why bring all the rest of us with you?" said Mrs. Brown. "As things have turned out it would have been far better watching the rain through our living room windows instead of sitting in your car getting all steamed up."

"*Our* car," said Mr. Brown. "And it seemed like a good idea at the time. The sun was shining and it felt like a typical Saturday afternoon with everybody at a loose end, so I thought we could combine things and kill two birds with one stone.

"I reckoned without the English summer weather."

Reaching into an inside pocket of his jacket, he produced an envelope and held it up for all to see. Clearly it was important, for the address was printed in black.

"It's my Income Tax Demand Note," he explained gloomily. "It's a last reminder that payment is due no later than Monday. I'm already in the Revenue's bad books for being late with the money last year. Two years running and they'll be putting a tag on me, and we shall all suffer."

"It would have been a help if we'd ended

up somewhere within walking distance of a pillar box," said Mrs. Brown.

Mr. Brown heaved a sigh. "On a day like today you might just as well say it would have been a help if the 'powers that be' had erected one right where we are, Mary, but they didn't.

"It's sheer lack of foresight. Remind me to write a letter of complaint when we get back home pointing out the error of their ways. They could put one every ten yards or so while they are at it."

"Sarcasm won't get you off the hook, Henry," said Mrs. Brown. "If your letter is so important you had better put a brave face on things and make a run for it."

"And get my new jacket sopping wet," said Mr. Brown. "I should cocoa!"

From his position in the back of the car Paddington caught the word "cocoa" and pricked up his ears.

"I didn't know we were having a picnic, Mr. Brown," he called excitedly. "I've never had a picnic in a car before. It's a good job I put a fresh marmalade sandwich under my hat before we came out."

"Shh!" hissed Judy. "We're not having a picnic now. You heard what Dad said. We're marooned and it's all a fault of the weather. Nobody is to blame.

"We are victims of circumstances," she continued dramatically. "The sun was shining when we left home, so we've all come out without our waterproofs. If it doesn't ease off, we could be sitting here for the rest of the afternoon."

"All except Paddington," broke in Jonathan.

"What do you mean?" said Judy. "All except Paddington?"

"Well," said Jonathan. "At least he's wearing his duffle coat, and Mrs. Bird was saying only the other day it was in need of a clean. If Paddington goes out in this downpour to post the letter, it will amount to him killing two birds with one stone—Mrs. Bird and Dad will both be happy."

He lowered his voice. "And I daresay

Paddington himself will be rewarded."

"Undoubtedly!" came a voice from the front of the car. "Good deeds should never go unrewarded. And when it's raining as hard as it is at the moment it deserves twice as much. What a splendid idea."

"It sounds very good value, Mr. Brown," said Paddington. "But I'm a bit worried about my whiskers. When it rains very hard the water runs down to the ends and it's got nowhere else to go."

"Don't let that worry you, Paddington," called Mr. Brown. "We can't allow that to happen. The boot of the car is unlocked. If it's of any help whisker-wise you can take one of the umbrellas."

Without further ado he handed the all-important letter over his shoulder.

"Whatever else you do, promise faithfully to guard it with your life."

"Thank you very much, Mr. Brown," said Paddington gratefully. "I will." And having made up his mind at long last, he followed

Mrs. Brown's example and rubbed a hole in the nearest steamed up window with the back of the paw to see if the weather was as bad at his end of the car as it was at the front.

As he pressed his nose against the glass he nearly jumped out of his skin with alarm when he found himself face-to-face with a man wearing a helmet. He was only inches

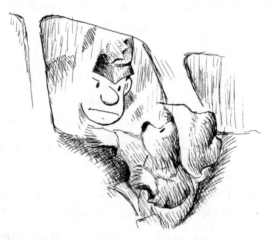

away from the glass, but there was no mistaking a figure of the law.

He must have been trying to see inside Mr. Brown's car, and he clearly felt unhappy at being caught out, so Paddington felt obliged to raise his hat in order to make him feel better. He received a salute in return.

Unaware of what was going on, Mr. Brown called out another warning. "Whatever you do, Paddington, don't get my letter mixed up with your marmalade sandwich. That's something else the Inland Revenue won't take kindly to—a sticky check. And I know who would get the blame."

"If I were you, Paddington," said Jonathan, as the policeman backed further away, "I'd use the door on the other side of the car, otherwise he'll keep you talking and you'll never get going. Besides, if Dad's letter gets sopping wet, bang goes your reward for doing a good deed."

Paddington needed no second bidding. One way and another, he was only too pleased to make good his escape; and having put Mr. Brown's letter under his hat for safekeeping, he was out of the car like a streak of lightning.

Jonathan and Judy heard the sound of

rummaging going on behind them, followed by a clunk as the door to the boot slammed shut. Moments later what looked for all the world like a large, brightly colored tent went past the window.

"Oh, dear," said Judy, "Dad won't be too pleased. That's his best golfing umbrella."

"At least with all those red, white, and blue stripes we shan't lose sight of him," said Jonathan.

"Perhaps it's just as well," said Judy. "With

it only half open he looks like an upside-down Knickerbocker Glory. Let's hope he doesn't open it fully. In this weather he's just as likely to get blown off his feet and end up like Mary Poppins."

The words were hardly out of her mouth when they heard a loud knocking on the driver's side at the front of the car.

"That's torn it," said Jonathan. "It's the copper who was lurking round the back. The one Paddington just raised his hat to. Dad's really not going to like it."

They both fell silent as their father wound his window down in response to the latest arrival.

"Are you aware, sir," said the man, "you have a bear in the back of your car?"

"A bear?" repeated Mr. Brown, playing for time. He looked over his shoulder. "What makes you think that? I can't see one."

"I know what I saw," said the policeman stubbornly. "Wearing a red hat, it was. Made a gesture towards me, he did. Like he was trying to raise it. Perhaps you wouldn't mind getting out of your car for a moment, sir . . ."

"Yes, I would mind," said Mr. Brown. "Apart from the fact that it's patently obvious there isn't a bear in the back of the car, even if there were it isn't a crime."

The policeman looked pained. "I had your best interests at heart," he said. "It could have escaped from the zoo for all you know."

"Careful, Henry," whispered Mrs. Brown. "He's only doing his job. Besides, he can't be from the local brigade. They all know Paddington by now."

"He's probably been drafted in to help with the Portobello Market," Jonathan hissed. "It's in all the papers. The traders are holding a gigantic all-day carnival."

"*Were* holding one must be the word by now," broke in Judy. "That's probably why all the roads are blocked."

"That's as may be . . ." began Mr. Brown, and then paused as the policeman, clearly intending to try his luck elsewhere, pocketed his notebook, and set off with a determined air, only to collide head-on with Paddington going in the opposite direction.

By now the windscreen was sufficiently clear of moisture to accommodate a view of the encounter, but it was only momentary. A split second later and it might never have happened as they toppled out of sight.

Despite frantic cleaning with anything that came to hand, moments passed before the side windows of the car were clear enough to see through, and although it revealed a grim-faced policeman talking into his mobile phone, Paddington was nowhere to be seen.

"Would you believe it?" said Jonathan. "Mrs. Bird's favorite motto is *'Bears always fall on their feet.'* He must have done it again."

"He didn't have your father's envelope in his paw at the time, thank goodness," said Mrs. Brown.

"He had it under his hat to keep it dry," said Judy. "And I bet that survived the accident. There's a lot to be said for an old Government Surplus bush hat."

"All he's got to do now is find the nearest pillar box," said Jonathan.

The Browns fell silent. From time to time a policeman or two floated past like phantoms, until suddenly the chatter of raised voices broke the monotony.

"Typical!" said Mr. Brown. "The rain's easing off."

"Shh!" hissed Mrs. Brown. "I think they are arguing about something."

"I said I don't like the sound of it," repeated a voice, almost as though he was doing it for her benefit. "You know that vertically challenged foreign guy who wanted to post a letter . . ."

"The one who couldn't reach the slot to drop it in so you offered to do it for him," shouted another. "Bit rude I thought. Making you lift him up just so he got to drop the letter in himself. He wouldn't let go of it."

"Oh, he was polite enough," said the first speaker. "Raised his hat and even said 'thank you' when I put him down. It was what he said afterwards that bothers me . . . 'I had to do it myself because *I promised to guard it with my life*'!"

There was a pause while the words sank in, followed almost immediately by a stream of voices anxious to climb on the bandwagon. "It struck me he was a bit suspect," said one.

"He told me he used to belong to an outfit in South America called *The Home for Retired Bears*," agreed another. "It sounds like some kind of gang."

"Run by a woman called Aunt Lucy," broke in a third. "Sounds like a nasty piece of work. He had to report to her regularly."

"The word 'marmalade' kept cropping up," added someone else. "It could be a code word of some kind."

"Maybe we could get the Post Office to retrieve the envelope," suggested someone else.

Mr. Brown's groan was barely complete when to his relief the idea was quashed as being too time consuming.

"We need to move in as speedily and quietly as possible," said an authoritative voice. "Now, here's what I suggest . . ."

His words were a cue for the general lowering of voices, and try as they might, the Browns had to admit defeat.

"You can say one thing for Paddington," said Mr. Brown. "Shyness isn't his middle name."

"He's certainly made his presence felt on this occasion," said Mrs. Brown. "I don't know what his Aunt Lucy will think if she gets to hear she's been classed as the leader of a gang . . ."

She paused as two members out of a small group of policemen broke away from the others and headed in their direction.

"Meanwhile, it looks as though we may have company."

"Two is not good news, I'm afraid," said Mr. Brown.

"I bet there will be a nice one to keep Dad talking," said Jonathan, "while the other one does his best to find something wrong with the car."

"Lesson number one in the Brown School of Motoring," murmured Judy, as her father opened his door in readiness for their arrival.

As it happened, when they arrived they were clearly intent on getting down to work straight away. "This is the car the bear was in," said the leader, "and this gentleman was denying all knowledge of it."

"I was doing no such thing," said Mr. Brown. "I simply said he wasn't sitting in the backseat of our car any longer."

"Another thing," said the policeman, ignoring Mr. Brown's response, "we would like all the windows open."

"Certainly not," said Mr. Brown. "I have my family to think of, and it's getting cold in here. As I'm sure you are only too well aware, it's against the law to leave your engine running when you are parked for any length of time . . ."

The two policemen exchanged glances.

"I'm afraid it's an order," said the policeman. He took out his notebook. "Talking of things being against the law, you do realize, I suppose, that you are parked on a double yellow line. Not only is that forbidden at any time of the day or night even if there are no upright signs, but I could have you down for loitering with intent."

"Intent to do what?" asked Mr. Brown.

"That," said the policeman, "is what we must look into."

"Have you seen the state of this gentleman's nearside front tire?" asked the second policeman. "A good kick is all it needs."

"That's the one who checks the car," whispered Jonathan in the back seat.

The words were hardly out of his mouth before the officer stepped back and by way of proof, drew his right leg back and administered a hefty kick.

There was a hiss of escaping air and the Browns' car slowly tilted over to one side, carrying its occupants with it.

Jonathan nudged Judy. "See what I mean," he said.

"Awesome!" she exclaimed.

"Thanks a heap," said Mr. Brown.

"Shh, Henry." Mrs. Brown struck a warning note. "Why don't you try counting up to ten?"

"I don't envy you changing your spare wheel in this weather, sir," said the first policeman sympathetically.

"Fortunately that doesn't arise," said Mr. Brown. "I haven't got one with me."

"Ah!" The policeman licked the business end of his pencil. "Traveling without a spare wheel? Oh, dear me, sir!"

"It so happens I'm not traveling anywhere," said Mr. Brown.

"You're right there," said the second policeman. "Wait till the Superintendent back at the station hears about this. You will be able to produce the relevant documents, of course. Driving license. Insurance. Three yearly roadworthiness certificate, otherwise . . ."

"You don't know our Superintendent," said Mr. Brown. "I've played golf with him. He even shouts at the ball if it doesn't go into the hole cleanly. I hardly think he's going to laugh his head off when he hears how you kicked my front tire with such a force all the air came out. I draw the line about using the word 'vandalism,' but I wouldn't like to be in your shoes."

The group fell silent for a moment or two and then sprang into life as a familiar figure carrying a rolled umbrella came into view.

"Everybody out," said the policeman. "And that's an order. This is the one we want to question. He gave us the slip back at the postbox and it's not going to happen a second time."

And without further ado the two policemen occupied the front of the car, and seeing Jonathan and Judy alighting from the back, Paddington assumed they were making room for him and made for his old seat.

"Don't open the umbrella whatever you do, Paddington," called Mrs. Brown. "It's unlucky to open one indoors," she added for the benefit of the others. "I imagine the same thing applies to a car."

But she was too late. Paddington had already pressed the catch in the handle and as the folds of the umbrella unfurled, so water cascaded over the other occupants.

"If you ask me," said the first policeman, when the fuss died down. "It's a case of even-stevens. Bob's your uncle, Mr. Brown!"

"I didn't know you had an Uncle Bob, Mr. Brown," said Paddington, as he struggled with the catch on the umbrella. "Is he coming to stay? I'll be as quick as I can."

"Shh!" hissed Judy. "He hasn't. And no one is coming to stay."

Meanwhile, the second policeman reached a decision. "In the circumstances I'll stretch a point and call for a tow truck on my mobile," he said brusquely. "Wait here."

"We can hardly do anything else," said Mr. Brown.

"Neither can I," said the policeman, gritting his teeth.

It was much later that day before the Browns eventually arrived back home. It had stopped raining, and Mrs. Bird was waiting anxiously by the front door of Number thirty-two Windsor Gardens.

"Whatever kept you?" she asked.

"It's a long story," said Mrs. Brown.

"Has it got anything to do with bears?" asked Mrs. Bird.

The Browns stared at her. It really was uncanny the way her mind worked. Nothing got past her eagle eyes.

"It seems it was at its worst in this particular area," continued Mrs. Bird. She turned to Paddington. "Talking of which, what *have* you been doing to your duffle coat? It looks as though it's been to the cleaners."

"Thereby hangs a tale," said Mr. Brown.

"One we are doing our best to forget," said Mrs. Brown.

"News travels fast in this day and age," said Mrs. Bird. "It's in the evening paper, and it's been on the radio. I daresay you remember those storms we had a while back when everything got covered with a film of dust, and it turned out a lot of it came from the Sahara desert? Well, this time it's bears. Apparently it's been raining bears from Darkest Peru.

"There's a rumor going around that it may have something to do with the traders in the Portobello Market drumming up publicity for their carnival, which has been a bit of a washout with all the rain we've had, and I was wondering if it was nearer home than that . . ."

"Have they got any photographs?" asked Jonathan.

"I haven't seen any so far," said Mrs. Bird.

"Nor will you," said Judy. "Bears may come and bears may go, but there's only one Paddington," she added loyally. "Even he can't be in two places at once. If you ask me, someone, somewhere, is putting two and two together, and making a great deal too much of it."

"I couldn't agree more," said Mrs. Bird. "Mark my words, it will be another nine days' wonder. I think Paddington had better keep out of the way for the time being."

With that, she set about getting the supper ready, and it wasn't until later that evening that Mr. Brown remembered the promised award of a "little something" for Paddington posting his letter to the Income Tax Office.

He had already gone up to his room by then, and Mr. Brown followed him upstairs, only to find him sitting up in bed wearing a long white beard from his disguise outfit.

"Don't worry, Mr. Brown," he called. "It's me . . . Paddington!"

"Thank you for telling me," said Mr. Brown gravely. "I would never have guessed."

He waited while Paddington put the finishing touches to his disguise before handing him the money. "Don't spend it all at once," he said. "I think perhaps you should stay indoors for the next nine days or so until the fuss dies down anyway.

"Being photographed wherever you go is one thing if you are a famous film star, but it's something else again if you are a bear and like a quiet life. Practically everyone with a mobile telephone has a camera in it these days."

Paddington looked downcast behind his

beard. "Fancy not being able to go out for nine days," he said. "I shall miss my elevenses with Mr. Gruber. I don't know what he will have to say about it."

"Exactly the same as what I am about to say, I imagine," said Mr. Brown. "It's only a saying in much the same way as you say a cat has nine lives or someone is dressed up to the nines.

"Far from being closeted for exactly nine days, I suggest that in two or three days' time and a change in the weather it will be nothing more than a memory."

Paddington considered the matter for a moment or two. "Thank you very much for my 'little something,' Mr. Brown."

"There is a saying for that too," said Mr. Brown. "Possession is nine points of the law."

Paddington cheered up. "I think nine is a very nice number," he said. "When I do go out I shall buy nine buns for our elevenses. Mr. Gruber will be surprised."

Chapter Two

A BIRD IN THE HAND

One morning, some weeks after the epi-
sode with Mr. Brown's letter to the Income
Tax people, Paddington woke to the plaintive
chirping of a robin redbreast outside his bed-
room window.

Apart from the fact that it was earlier than usual, there was nothing untoward about it. As Mr. Brown was fond of saying, a garden isn't a garden without a robin redbreast to keep an eye on things. And it was true; he only had to apply a spade or a fork to a flower bed for it to appear in search of a worm or two. And just lately, probably because he was around more than his father, the robin had shown more than a passing interest in Paddington's activities.

In fact, ever since Paddington had been given a corner of the garden to call his own, he had never been short of a daily visit, and it often sang to him late into the night.

In a funny kind of way it sounded as though his feathered friend was trying to tell him something special. There was an urgent note to its chirrup, so he got out of bed to see what it could possibly be.

According to his best friend, Mr. Gruber, another thing about robin redbreasts was they were always first in line to herald the arrival of spring, and sure enough, when Paddington looked up at the sky there were several patches of blue in among the clouds, and the largest one of all was directly above Number thirty-two Windsor Gardens.

After the many long weeks of rain clouds they'd had to put up with, it seemed almost too good to be true, so there was no question of his going back to bed.

So, having thanked his visitor, Paddington passed a flannel over his own face, gave his whiskers a quick going over, and donned his duffle coat before hurrying downstairs as fast as he could in order to tell the others.

But either the robin had beaten him to it, or the rest of the family had been listening to the weather forecast on television, for according to Mrs. Bird, Mr. Brown had already left for his office, Mrs. Brown was out doing some early morning shopping, and even their bad-tempered neighbor, Mr. Curry, was up and about.

Apparently he had given Mrs. Bird a cheery wave over the fence that morning while casually asking after the state of their garden, which was most unusual, and deep down, although she didn't put it into words, she felt was rather suspect.

"There's nothing like a spot of sunshine to put a smile on people's faces and get things moving," she said. And to show it wasn't simply idle chatter on her part, she opened a fresh jar of her special homemade marmalade for Paddington to have with his breakfast.

"Thank you so much, Mrs. Bird," said Paddington. "It's very kind of you." He couldn't help noticing it was labeled 2014, which was a very good year.

And to show how grateful he was, he disposed of the entire contents in one go on the remains of the toast, and then washed the jar spotlessly clean afterwards.

"Mercy me!" exclaimed Mrs. Bird, when she saw what had happened. It wasn't quite

what she'd had in mind, but not wishing to spoil such a lovely day she kept her feelings to herself.

"Perhaps you ought to go for a run round the garden?" she suggested. "It will do you the world of good. Although, if you want my advice, I should keep your duffle coat on. There is an old saying, but a very true one: 'Ne'er cast a clout till May be out.' That means you shouldn't take the warm weather for granted. No matter what your robin redbreast has to say, it's still only the beginning of April, so it may not last."

After his mammoth breakfast, going for

a run round the garden wasn't exactly what Paddington had in mind either. Going back to bed would have been nearer the mark, but the Browns' housekeeper held the kitchen door firmly open for him, so he didn't have any choice in the matter.

He toyed with the idea of having a quick lie down on the lawn, but the grass hadn't been mown all the winter and on close inspection it didn't look very inviting. He was also beginning to realize the wisdom of keeping his duffle coat on, because despite the sunshine there was still a chill in the air. So before doing anything else, he set to work making sure all the toggles were securely fastened.

It was a bit difficult with paws, and he was still fumbling with the top one when Mrs. Bird opened the back door again.

"I didn't mean jogging on the spot," she said. "I meant running up and down the garden." And since he could feel her eyes following his progress—or lack of it from that moment on—he decided there was nothing

for it but to follow her instructions and carry on down to the end of the garden. If he did nothing else he could at least inspect his own plot in the far corner to see how it had survived the winter.

"I'm glad I didn't cast any clouts, Mrs. Bird," he called as the top toggle slipped into place at long last and he set off down the garden path.

The rockery was a present from Mr. Brown,

who was a keen gardener, and for most of the previous summer it had been Paddington's pride and joy.

It didn't cover a vast area. It wasn't, in fact, much larger than their dining room table, but there was a lot of truth in another of Mr. Brown's sayings: "There is always work to do in the garden, even if it's only the size of a window box," and he had helped Paddington build a rockery which occupied a good half of it.

There had been a robin redbreast around then, although not the same one, of course. Paddington had planted some sunflower seeds from a packet of free ones in a magazine belonging to Mrs. Brown, and in no time at all they had grown so much they were twice as tall as he was, so Mr. Brown set about advising him on what plants he should buy and where to plant them, without once suggesting it should come out of his pocket money.

Thanks to his advice, the following spring had been spectacularly successful. Even Mr.

Curry had passed some admiring glances at it over the fence when it was in full bloom.

To help him remember which plants were which, Jonathan had given him some specially made metal name tabs with his own name on the back for his summer birthday present.

It was a very kind thought, because most of the plants had very complicated names. For example, the one he thought of as a duffle-coat blue was a *Veronica pectinata*, and the one that matched his bush hat was a dwarf phlox, *Temiscaming,* which he had a job to pronounce, let alone spell. There was a yellow plant which was a *Saxifraga* called *berseriana*.

Paddington liked the sound of that one, and he often dropped it into the conversation when it turned to the subject of gardening.

The man in the nursery where Paddington bought them all had been most impressed. "We don't get many bear customers," he said. "I suppose being so near the ground helps."

As Paddington approached his garden he

saw there was a solitary thrush perched on one of the rocks, but it flew off as soon as it caught sight of him. Apart from that there was no sign of life whatsoever. In fact, it looked a shambles, and he wondered if the foxes had been at it. Mrs. Bird had been out with her umbrella chasing them off the property several times of late, and there had been talk of a number of cubs in the area. He wouldn't put it past them.

Taking a closer look at the rockery he decided most of the earth must have been washed away during the recent downpour, along with many of the smaller plants that hadn't had time to take root. Even the name tags were missing. Instead of the blaze of color he'd been hoping for it was a sorry mess.

While he was staring at the remains of the rockery, his robin redbreast landed close by to see what was going on.

"That's where I planted my *Saxifraga berseriana*," said Paddington hotly as it dug its beak into the nearest hole. "Now look at it!"

The robin glanced up at him noncommittally, but before he had a chance to say any more they both heard a strange noise coming from the next garden.

It sounded like someone cutting some rusty bits of tin. Either that or the foxes were on the prowl again. If not, then it had to be Mr. Curry himself, which was hard to picture.

The Browns' neighbor wasn't an early riser at the best of times, and even if he had waved at Mrs. Bird that very morning, he had never been known to do any work in his garden until much later in the day, if then.

The sound of sawing was punctuated every so often by growls of disappointment. Clearly, all was not well, although there was nothing new in that; Mr. Curry wasn't noted for his prowess as a "do-it-yourself" addict, but it was rather early in the day for such loud displays of bad temper, even for him.

Paddington stood the flow of noises-off for as long as possible while he searched in vain for any signs of growth on his rockery. Then, following a louder than ever bellow, he was unable to contain his curiosity a moment longer.

Abandoning his search for the slightest sign of a green shoot, he made his way to the fence dividing the two gardens one from the other and peered through a convenient knothole.

Chapter Three

CURRY'S THE NAME

Sure enough, although Mr. Curry wasn't exactly doing a war dance, the top half of him was leaping up and down brandishing a saw. To say something was not to his liking was putting it mildly. If it had been possible to cut the air around him into little pieces, there would have been a large pile of it lying at his feet, awaiting the arrival of a dustcart.

In the hope of getting a better view, Paddington fetched a garden chair.

"Bear!" bellowed Mr. Curry accusingly, as he caught sight of Paddington's head appearing above the top of the fence. "Spying on me again, are you!"

"Oh, no, Mr. Curry," said Paddington hastily. "I was just trying to get a better view. It's a bit difficult to see properly through a knothole, and I thought you might be in trouble and need help."

Mr. Curry's eyes narrowed. "May I ask what you are doing in the garden at this early hour?"

"I was checking my rockery," said Paddington. "But there's nothing to see except a lot of holes. I think the foxes may have dug them up."

"Foxes!" exclaimed Mr. Curry. "Don't mention the word. Look at my lawn. It's full of holes."

"I didn't know you had a lawn, Mr. Curry," said Paddington.

"Well, there you are," said Mr. Curry. "That shows how bad things are. And then there's the rain. We've had so much recently the ground has become like a marsh. Your side of the fence is all right. You have a patio, but I've only got earth on my side."

Mr. Curry glared at him. "If you must know," he said, "I'm having trouble with my legs. They weren't too good in the first place, but with all the wet weather we've been having the ground is as rough as can be, so I'm cutting bits off to even things up."

Paddington nearly fell off the chair in a state of shock at the news. He stared at the Browns' neighbor. "You've been cutting bits off your legs?" he said. "No wonder you've been making funny noises."

"What do you mean, bear?" barked Mr. Curry.

"Well," said Paddington. "It must be very painful cutting bits off them. Mind you, Mrs. Bird will be pleased. She often says you are too tall for your own good; always looking over the top of our fence to see what's going on. I expect you could borrow her First Aid box."

"Bah!" growled Mr. Curry. "I'll give her First Aid."

"I don't think she needs any at the moment,"

said Paddington. "She was all right the last time I saw her."

He took a closer look at the scene next door but he couldn't see any signs of blood on Mr. Curry's saw or, for that matter, rivulets coming out from under his trouser legs. It was rather disappointing.

"Perhaps you ought to see a doctor?" he suggested. "Or I could have a go for you. Bears are good at sawing."

Mr. Curry's eyes narrowed again. "It isn't easy," he said. "It's like I keep saying. Your side of the fence is all right. You have a patio, but I've only got plain earth on my side. Now it's gone hard again all my garden furniture . . . the table . . . the chairs . . . has got the wobbles."

"And now your legs have gone wibbly-woo too?" suggested Paddington, hoping for a demonstration.

"I wouldn't put it quite like that," said the Browns' neighbor casually. He eyed Paddington thoughtfully. "But I must admit I could do with some help with my sawing. A little evening up of the legs on my table and chairs for a start wouldn't come amiss. It would be good practice for you."

It didn't take more than a moment or two for Paddington to make up his mind. "I might have to cast off some of my clouts," he said. "You can't do sawing wearing a duffle coat. I must ask Mrs. Bird what she thinks before I do anything because it isn't May yet."

"I don't know about your clouts, bear," said Mr. Curry dubiously, "but you won't be needing a duffle coat. I'll tell you that for a start. Besides, I would rather you didn't tell anyone else about this for the time being, least of all Mrs. Bird. Let it be a nice surprise for them."

And without further ado, he helped Paddington over the fence into his garden. "It so happens I have some important business to attend to this morning. That's why I was up earlier than usual. But if I leave you to get on with it and you do a good job we'll see what we can do in the way of a reward at the end of the day."

As Paddington opened his mouth to respond, the Browns' neighbor put a finger to his lips. "There's no need to say 'thank you, Mr. Curry' just yet," he said. "And remember—not a word to anyone, or you won't get a reward."

With that, he turned on his heels and disappeared into his house.

Paddington decided Mr. Curry's legs must either heal very quickly or he had removed very small chunks so far, for there wasn't the slightest sign of a limp.

A few moments later he heard the front door slam, so he gave a sigh and set to work with the saw. Much to his surprise, it went through the wood like a hot knife through butter and he soon had a small pile of wood by his side.

It wasn't long before his robin redbreast turned up. It was having a field day and no

mistake, but clearly didn't think much of Paddington's sawing, so it soon disappeared.

Meanwhile, Mrs. Brown had returned from her shopping.

"What's up with Mr. Curry today?" she said. "I passed him in the street and he was beaming like someone who's won a fortune on the football pools!"

"It's the sunshine," said Mrs. Bird. "I even got a wave from him this morning. Mind you, if you ask me he's up to something. He's got Paddington sawing up his old garden furniture for him. Goodness knows how."

"Or why?" said Mrs. Brown. "Perhaps he's running short of firewood."

"I can't help thinking there's something more to it than that," said Mrs. Bird. "Meanwhile, it's keeping Paddington occupied and that's no bad thing. He could do with losing a bit of weight round the middle."

"I can't hear anything," said Mrs. Brown.

"It's time for his elevenses with Mr. Gruber," said Mrs. Bird. "He won't want to miss that."

The Browns' housekeeper had put her finger on one reason for Paddington's absence, little dreaming there were others, more pressing.

"I'm intrigued," said Mrs. Brown. "Shall we take a quick look while no one else is about?" Without waiting for an answer, she led the way into the garden.

"Heavens above!" she exclaimed as she

looked over the top of the fence. "I don't believe it. I just don't believe it. Tell me it isn't true."

"I wish, I wish!" said Mrs. Bird, as she joined her. "I wish I could tell you it isn't. But there's no getting away from the fact that it is. There for all to see."

They both fell silent as they gazed at the result of Paddington's labors.

Much to his credit, everything was very tidy. All the sawn-off pieces of wood had been put in a neat pile, and all four chairs were in place around the table. The only thing wrong with it was that in his anxiety to make a good job, Paddington must have had so many goes at trying to get rid of their wobbles the legs were now so short the seats were only about three inches off the ground.

"Mr. Curry's not going to like it," said Mrs. Brown.

"I daresay it'll wipe the smile off his face," agreed Mrs. Bird. "I knew it was too good to be true.

"Perhaps Mr. Gruber will know what to do next," she added hopefully. "He usually turns up trumps."

And indeed he did. For when Paddington returned, suitably refreshed by his cocoa and buns, he immediately set to work cutting the legs off the table by an equal amount to the chair legs so that when everything was in place it became a garden feature. He had even given Paddington a set of wooden gnomes to provide a finishing touch.

Short of gluing everything back together there was no going back on the idea, and it was with some trepidation that Mrs. Brown and Mrs. Bird awaited the return of Mr. Curry.

But much to everyone's relief, the Browns' neighbor seemed so pleased with the way things had turned out he not only gave Paddington a shilling for his pains but he had everything transfered to his front garden, and all next day he was to be heard pottering about with it behind a hastily erected screen.

"Wonders will never cease," said Mrs. Brown.

"There's a first time for everything," said Mrs. Bird darkly. "You mark my words."

They hadn't long to wait, for the following day was a Saturday and when the boy arrived with the daily paper he happened to bump into Mr. Brown as he opened the front door.

"Not going in for the competition this year, Mr. Brown?" he said cheerfully.

"Competition?" repeated Mr. Brown. "What competition?"

"The Best Spring Front Garden competition," said the boy. "It's run by the local council to make up for the bad winter we had. And today's the day. There's some good prizes to be had. I delivered the leaflets some weeks ago. Put one in every door on my round except yours. Your neighbor said he would save me the trouble. Don't tell me he didn't give it to you?"

Mr. Brown glanced across at the house next door. There was no sign of Mr. Curry, and whatever he had been up to in his front garden was covered over with a sheet.

He hadn't seen the arrangement of tables and chairs for himself, but from all he had heard he couldn't picture it winning any major prizes. An award for originality, perhaps . . . but no more.

He turned back to the paperboy. "Have you any idea what time judging starts?"

"This afternoon," said the boy. "Two o'clock onwards."

"Would you care to earn a few bob?"

"Wouldn't I just!" exclaimed the boy.

"Done!" said Mr. Brown. Swiveling round in a half-circle he stuck his head into the hall. "Paddington!" he shouted. "There's work to be done. Drop everything."

There was a distant crash of breaking china, but in the excitement it was soon forgotten.

There were the roses to give a last-minute late second pruning, begonias in pots to titivate—both Mr. Brown's pride and joy. Gravel to rake free of weeds. It was a combined effort to make it look at its pristine best.

Then, after lunch there was a ring at the front door bell, and Mr. Gruber put in an appearance. Having shut up shop for the afternoon, he had come to see how things were going, and he was just in time because the council party had reached next door and Mr. Curry was removing the cover on his entry.

There was a universal sinking of hearts at number thirty-two, for despite all their hard work, compared with their entry, his was undoubtedly a blaze of color.

"The old rogue," said Mrs. Brown. "He's copied Paddington's rockery."

"To a tee," agreed Mr. Brown. "Would you believe it?"

Paddington took a closer look. "I think they're *my* plants!" he exclaimed hotly. "That's my *Saxifraga berseriana*. I planted it myself last year." He pointed to a cluster of flowers. "I put it next to that dufflecoat blue plant."

At that moment, almost as though dead on cue, there was a fluttering of wings and a newcomer arrived on the scene. Having landed like a tiny helicopter alongside Paddington's finger, it dug its beak into the spot he was pointing to.

"May I see that?" said the judge, noticing a gleam of metal.

"*Veronica pectinata*," he read out loud. "*And it has a name and address printed on the back: Paddington Bear, 32 Windsor Gardens.*"

He turned to address Mr. Curry, but the Browns' neighbor was nowhere to be seen.

"I was right all the time," said Mrs. Bird triumphantly. "I said it was probably the work of a fox. Nasty creatures; always on the prowl—chancing their luck in the hope of getting something for nothing."

"Well," said the judge, casting a benevolent eye over the Browns' immaculate garden, "that being the case, and since the ownership of the flowers in this display seems to be divided between the two houses, I can only suggest the first prize for the best front garden should be divided between the two."

It was a popular decision which drew a round of applause from everyone present and caused the robin redbreast to take off.

After it was all over, amid general agreement, Mrs. Brown likened its arrival to the last-minute appearance through a gap in the hills of the cavalry in an old-time cowboy movie. "It was quite uncanny," she said. "I wouldn't have believed it if I hadn't seen it with my own eyes."

"Their hearts may be small," said Mr.

Gruber. "But they do say it can beat at one thousand times a minute when it's roused, and despite their size they can be quite aggressive if they feel their territorial rights are being invaded. On this occasion this includes Paddington, and rightly so."

"To sum up," said Mrs. Brown, "a friend in need is a friend indeed. And all because of the work of a few foxes."

"If you ask me," corrected Mrs. Bird. "There was only one and it didn't have far to go. I doubt you will ever catch it, because it goes into hiding when the going gets rough. Its name is Curry and it lives next door."

"Even old Curry wouldn't sink as low as that, would he?" said Mr. Brown. "Stealing a young bear's rockery garden!"

"He did his best to make sure we didn't even know about the competition in the first place," said Mrs. Bird.

And really, there was little more to be said.

Chapter Four

PADDINGTON'S
MAGICAL MOMENTS

"I didn't know it's Mr. Gruber's birthday in two weeks' time," said Mrs. Brown.

"Neither did I," said Mrs. Bird. "Where did you hear that?"

"Paddington told me," said Mrs. Brown.

"Apparently they were talking about his early life in Hungary over elevenses in his shop the other day, and during the conversation Mr. Gruber let fall the fact that he would never forget the date because it happens to fall on what is a national holiday in that part of the world.

"He didn't say any more than that, but Paddington looked it up in one of Jonathan's old diaries that lists such things, and he says it must be May the twenty-sixth, which happens to fall on a Saturday this year."

"Perhaps we should ask him to tea," said Mrs. Bird.

"It's the very least we can do," said Mrs. Brown. "I doubt if he has anything planned. If it wasn't for the shop there's nobody else in his life, and he's been so good to Paddington over the years. I don't know what that bear would do without him. Jonathan and Judy can come for the weekend, and Henry can forgo his golf for once. I vote we pull the stops out and throw a party for him."

Mrs. Brown's enthusiasm was infectious, and one thing rapidly led to another. So when Jonathan came across a paperback publication called *The Jumbo Book of Party Tricks* he immediately put it in the post for Paddington to see.

"I don't like the look of that," said Mrs. Bird as she spotted him passing her kitchen window immersed in its pages. "That bear knows quite enough tricks as it is. He's already asked if he can have a sheet hanging across the doorway between the hall and the living room where the party is taking place."

"I'll tell you something else," said Mrs. Brown. "Mr. Curry was looking over our fence a moment ago and I think he's spotted something special is going on. I wouldn't mind betting he'll be inviting himself along, too, and that'll spoil everything. You mark my words."

Indeed, Mr. Gruber's face fell when he arrived at Number thirty-two Windsor Gardens at the appointed time the following afternoon and found the Browns' neighbor already occupying the seat of honor, but he was much too polite to say anything.

"There's only one thing nicer than a cake fresh from the oven," said Mr. Curry, helping himself from a plate on the table, "and that's two. Tell that bear to hurry up. I'm hungry and I haven't got all day."

The Browns exchanged unhappy glances, but before Mr. Brown had a chance to say anything, the sheets hanging across the hall doorway parted and Paddington appeared.

"Good afternoon, Ladies and Gentlemen and Mr. Curry," he said, amid applause. "And a very special welcome to our special guest, Mr. Gruber.

"I would like to begin with a song," he continued.

"Oh, dear," said Mrs. Brown. "Is that wise?"

"I shall do it without moving my lips," said Paddington firmly.

And the next moment he put one paw against his chest and launched into the first words of "Many brave hearts are asleep in the deep . . . deep . . . deep . . ."

"It's Dad's old wind-up gramophone," whispered Jonathan from behind the sheets.

"The needle must be stuck in a groove," agreed Judy.

"Not a very good start," grumbled Mr. Curry as Paddington disappeared behind the sheet in order to investigate matters. "I shall have another cake to make up for it."

They had rather a long wait, but when Paddington reappeared he was struggling with a long curtain rod which had a large black ball at both ends. When he finally came to rest, he first of all spent some moments mopping his brow and then bent down and grasped the middle of the rod with both paws.

Mrs. Bird watched anxiously as he struggled to lift the contraption. "I hope that bear doesn't do himself a mischief," she whispered.

But nobody in the audience dared to lend a helping hand, and it was left to Mr. Brown and Mr. Gruber to lead the applause as Paddington finally managed to raise the object above his head, and even Mr. Curry paused before reaching for another cake.

"Of course," he said grudgingly, "that's one advantage of being short. It didn't have far to go."

Reaching inside his duffle coat for a

handkerchief in order
to mop his brow again,
Paddington let go of the
rod and it floated gently
up to the ceiling.

"Fancy painting a pair
of toy balloons black and
pretending they weigh a
ton," snorted Mr. Curry.
He helped himself to yet
another cake. "I hope the
next trick's better. That
one didn't fool me for a
moment!"

"Oh, it will be, Mr.
Curry," said Paddington
earnestly. "You wait and
see."

The others watched
nervously as Padding-
ton piled the remaining
cakes onto a larger plate,

which he then balanced on top of his head. Having covered it with a cloth, he waved a magic wand in the air several times. Then, having uttered the word *"abracadabra!"* he removed the cloth.

"Goodness," said Mrs. Brown, "they've vanished!"

"And me out of flour!" said Mrs. Bird.

"The quickness of the paw deceives the eye," said Mr. Gruber.

"It wasn't *that* quick!" barked Mr. Curry suspiciously. "Besides, he's got cream all over his whiskers."

"Perhaps I could make you a cup of tea instead, Mr. Curry," said Paddington. "I'll put the kettle on."

When he returned he had a cup and saucer balanced on the end of a stick.

"That's the oldest trick in the world," growled Mr. Curry. "Gluing a cup and saucer together. Here—give me that—I'll show you . . ."

No one knew what happened next, but the bellow of rage from Mr. Curry as he made a dash for the door and the crash of breaking china said it all.

"Oh, dear!" Mrs. Brown surveyed the empty table. "It doesn't seem to have been much of a birthday party."

"Never mind," said Mr. Gruber. "I've enjoyed myself no end, and perhaps young Mr.

Brown has some more tricks up his sleeve."

"I've saved my best one until last," said Paddington. "I only hope my *abracadabra* worked."

So saying, he lifted up the cloth he had used earlier and lo and behold, there were the missing cakes!

"Which only goes to show," said Mr. Gruber, "the quickness of the paws certainly does deceive the eye."

"And still waters run deep," said Mrs. Bird. Her eagle eyes had just spotted a warning note in Paddington's book under the heading HOW TO GET RID OF AN UNWANTED VISITOR. It said: *Never use hot water on the china. It may make the glue melt.* "If you ask me there's more to that bear's *abracadabras* than meets anyone's eye."

Chapter Five

DINNER FOR ONE

"I do hope we're doing the right thing, Henry," said Mrs. Brown as she joined the rest of the family in front of the television set. "I feel all keyed up. Paddington's only been gone half an hour and already it feels like an eternity."

"*We're* not doing anything, Mary," said Mr. Brown. "For once he's only got himself to blame if anything goes wrong."

"At least they sent a car for him," said Jonathan.

"I can't see what all the fuss is about," said Mr. Brown. "It's only a cookery program after all, and they're two a penny these days."

"Dad!" Judy looked at her father pityingly. "It isn't only a cookery program. It's *Dinner for One*."

"It's only the best cookery program ever," agreed Jonathan. "It's broken all records. It topped over ten million viewers last week. Mind you, it wasn't on any of the sports pages, so you might have missed it."

"Well, I wouldn't mind a dinner for one myself," said Mr. Brown. "Half the office typing pool left off early today. That's why I'm late home."

"Don't worry, Henry," said Mrs. Brown. "Yours is in the oven keeping hot. Mrs. Bird's just checking to make sure it doesn't get burnt."

"I bet I know why they left off early," said Jonathan, nudging his sister. "The news has reached the City at long last."

"Ever since they raised the winnings they've been sitting up and taking notice," said Judy. "I'm surprised you haven't bought a few shares, Dad."

"Well they must be scraping the barrel a bit if they've invited Paddington to be on the program," replied Mr. Brown defensively. "That's all I can say."

"They didn't invite him," said Mrs. Brown. "That's the whole point of it. The contestants apply to be on it and Paddington's application was accepted."

"You mean he *applied*?" said Mr. Brown.

"He thought he would surprise us," said Judy. "I think his friend Mr. Gruber helped him when it came to filling up the form, but it was Paddington's idea. You know how keen he is on anything new, and there are some jolly big prizes to be won."

"Well, give him his due," said Mr. Brown

grudgingly. "Ten out of ten for that. But won't they be in for a bit of a shock? There can't be many bears taking part."

"There's a first time for everything," said Jonathan, "and you get all sorts going in for it. They must be used to it by now."

"The jury stays the same every week," explained Judy. "And there are six different contestants. After a brief chat with the panel to make them feel at home and say who they are and where they come from, they are each given a sealed box of ingredients."

"That part of it is pot luck," broke in Jonathan. "No two boxes are the same."

"Then they are led off to a cooking area," continued Judy, "where all the implements they will need to prepare a main course are ready and waiting, and given fifteen minutes to do it in. It's a real race against time. You wait until you see some of the dishes people come up with. It's an absolute hoot."

"In the meantime," said Mr. Brown, "I wouldn't mind being led off to our cooking area. Mrs. Bird must be getting lonely in the kitchen all by herself."

"Don't worry, Henry," said Mrs. Brown. "She'll be out of there like a shot as soon as the program starts. She won't want to miss a second of it."

The words had hardly left her mouth when a fanfare of trumpeters from the Household Cavalry heralded the start of the program, and as a banner inscribed DINNER FOR ONE fluttered from a mast and filled the screen, Mrs. Bird materialized.

"Don't worry," she whispered to Mrs. Brown. "Everything's on simmer."

Mr. Brown's murmur of "Sounds like the title of a book" fell on deaf ears as the opening preamble to the program came to an end and the picture on the screen changed to reveal a packed studio audience.

"Good Heavens!" exclaimed Mr. Brown, as to a round of frantic applause an aristocratic figure made his way down the center aisle and up onto the stage to greet the first of the contestants. "There's old Percy Rushmore."

"*Sir* Percival Rushmoor, spelt with two o's," said Mrs. Brown.

"There's a lot of money in cast-offs," murmured Mr. Brown. "Especially if you make friends with the right people. I wonder what became of his barrow?"

"Shh," hissed Mrs. Brown. "Don't spoil it for the others."

"That's Anne Gellica, the former TV

chef," said Judy, as there was a further round of applause when the camera zoomed in to a head-and-shoulders shot of an elderly lady wearing a chef's white toque hat.

"And that's Ron Keeps, the boxer," said Jonathan, as the camera panned to yet another figure. "It says in a paper I was reading the other day he has a steak for breakfast every day. Two if he has a fight on his hands the same evening."

Mr. Brown stifled a groan. "Don't rub it in," he murmured.

"This is my favorite," said Judy, as Ron Keeps shook one fist in the air and then stepped aside to reveal the flamboyant figure of Romney Marsh, the famous gourmet and art historian.

"He always judges a dish by its color," she said. "Anyone lucky enough to have a bottle of tomato ketchup in their kit is guaranteed another ten points."

"And that last one was Martin Goodbody QC," said Jonathan. "He's a famous lawyer and he's there to make sure there's no hanky-panky going on."

"Hanky-panky?" echoed Mr. Brown. "In a cookery program?"

"You'd be surprised," said Jonathan. "People trying to smuggle their own food in for starters. That kind of thing . . ."

"Not much gets past him," said Judy. "Someone brought an inflatable marrow in the other week and when he gave it a prod it went off with a bang and everything collapsed. The firemen came rushing on and sprayed the remains . . ."

She broke off as the cameraman zoomed out, and to renewed cheers from the audience a familiar figure dressed in a blue duffle coat and crumpled bush hat brought the arrival of the contestants to an end.

Paddington turned to face the audience and for a brief moment or two appeared to be trying to raise his hat, but to no avail. Seeing his predicament the program's host came to the rescue.

Hurrying forward, he held out a welcoming hand. "Sir Percival Rushmoor," he said, "I'm invigilating."

"I'm very sorry to hear that, Sir Percival," said Paddington. "I hope you feel better very soon."

Amid laughter from the audience he held out a paw. "Paddington Brown, from Darkest Peru."

"Don't tell me you've come all this way just for a cookery program," said Sir Percival. "Amazin'. If you find yourself out ridin' in the Cotswolds you must pop in and see me in the family home. You'd be most welcome."

"Thank you very much, Sir Percival," said Paddington. "I live in Windsor Gardens and it's on several bus routes. You would be very welcome there, I'm sure."

"Thanks a heap," said Mr. Brown. "How many people did you say watch this program?"

"Over ten million at the last count," said Jonathan.

"Thank goodness Paddington didn't give him the number of our house," said Mr. Brown. "We'd be besieged by photographers if he had."

"Er, thank you very much," said Sir Percival.

"I'll make a note of that. Before we begin, tell me, have you had much culinary experience? If so, what is your favorite dish?"

"Mrs. Bird lets me have a go sometimes," said Paddington. "And it's chocolate cake."

"How very interesting," said Sir Percival. "Why is that?"

"It doesn't show the dirt," said Paddington.

"Perhaps I won't come to tea after all," said Sir Percival amid renewed laughter. "And on that happy note I suggest we make a start on our own *Dinner for One*."

"I think I'll have mine on a tray if you don't mind, Mrs. Bird," said Mr. Brown as another fanfare of trumpets bellowed from the loudspeaker. "I wouldn't want to miss anything."

Judy nudged Jonathan. "What did I tell you?" she whispered. "It's catching."

"Glued to the screen if you ask me," agreed her brother as the contestants began queuing up to receive their sealed cardboard boxes.

"They are all different," he explained to his father. "Nobody knows what's inside them until they're opened. It's a case of pot luck."

"Pot luck's right," said Judy. "Most weeks there is usually someone who strikes lucky."

"Or unlucky," said Jonathan. "One of the contestants got lumbered with frogs' legs and custard powder the other week. Can you imagine?"

While they were talking a curtain at the back of the set rose to reveal a row of mini kitchens, each complete with a sink, electric grill, and all the basic tools deemed necessary to complete a main course in the shortest possible time. It was truly a test of culinary imagination, and any pretense that it was taking place somewhere other than a television studio disappeared as cameras appeared from all directions to take close-ups of the scene.

Some of the kitchens were full of activity from the word go; others were desperately lacking in any kind of movement.

Mrs. Bird made haste with Mr. Brown's

dinner. "I hope I haven't missed anything vital," she said, placing a tray on his lap. "How is he doing?"

"Hard to tell," replied Mr. Brown. "The cameras seem to be giving him a wide berth for some reason or other. They keep moving in to get as close as possible, then make a dash for it. Perhaps they aren't used to dealing with bears."

"Paddington's been giving them some very hard stares," said Mrs. Brown. "They probably want danger money."

"He seems to be talking to himself a lot," said Judy. "And he keeps wiping his whiskers. There must be something going on."

"There had better be," said Jonathan, looking at the dining-room clock. "He hasn't got long to go."

"Time!" said Mr. Brown. "The unseen enemy! If you want it to pass quickly, the clock seems to stand still. If you want to prolong the moment, it disappears before you can say the proverbial Jack Robinson. They ought to make this an hour-long program."

"It is," said Mrs. Brown.

"Well, two hours then," said Mr. Brown. "What better way to spend an evening?"

"I wish we knew what ingredients Paddington had in his box," said Mrs. Bird.

"*Had* is the right word," said Mrs. Brown shortly afterwards, when a bell indicated the time was up, and having waved their empty boxes towards the audience the contestants made their way single file towards the judges' rostrum. And once again Paddington was bringing up the rear. Worse still, whatever it was he had to show for his labors was on a plate covered over by a tea towel.

"Very sensible," said Mrs. Bird approvingly. "He doesn't want it to get cold."

"An even better method would have been to make sure he was first in the queue," said Mr. Brown. "My navarin stew was excellent, Mrs. Bird, by the way."

"Stews are what you are going to see from most of the other competitors, if you ask me," said Judy, as one by one they displayed their efforts and applause from the audience began to show distinct signs of having been prerecorded as it grew in volume rather than lessened, mostly in tell-tale sharp bursts.

At long last it was Paddington's turn, and everything went deadly quiet.

"Now," said Sir Percival. "First of all tell us what ingredients you had. Then show us what you did with them."

"Well," said Paddington, "I had some chicory. I know it was chicory because we had some only the other day. And I had a big carton of cream, and something big and black wrapped in tissue paper. That was all."

"So, what did you do with them?" asked Sir Percival.

"I grilled the chicory," said Paddington. "But only lightly. Mrs. Bird doesn't like me getting too near grills in case I singe my whiskers and they don't grow back again. Bears need them when they go through narrow doorways, you know."

"I didn't know that," admitted Sir Percival.

"Then I added all the cream and I sliced the black thing that was wrapped in tissue paper and added that too," continued Paddington. "It had a label saying *Tuber melanosporum* on the outside and it was very heavy."

"That wasn't any old black thing," said Martin Goodbody. "That was a truffle. It must be your lucky day."

"He can't possibly go wrong with ingredients like that, can he?" said Mr. Brown. "Good old Paddington!" he shouted at the television screen, while the others exchanged glances.

"I have said it before," said Mrs. Bird, "and at the risk of repeating myself, I'll say it again. 'Bears always fall on their feet.'"

"I used it all up," said Paddington. "Now I feel sick."

"I expect it's the perfume," said Mr. Goodbody. "It's very heady. I can smell it from here." He licked his lips.

"I can't wait to taste it," agreed Anne Gellica.

"I'm afraid there isn't any left," said Paddington.

There was a stunned silence.

"What do you mean, bear?" said Sir Percival. "*There isn't any left?*"

"I know just what Miss Gellica meant," said Paddington. "I couldn't wait to taste it either."

"Do you mean to say you have eaten all

of it?" exclaimed Sir Percival. "But you can't have."

"It was quite easy," said Paddington. "I'll show you how if you like. All you need is a knife and fork. Mind you, it's a bit difficult with paws, so I had to use a spoon."

He removed the napkin and held the plate up for the others to see. "I've licked it clean so you can use it again if you want to.

"It doesn't say anywhere in the instructions you can't eat it yourself," he added. "I thought I had better test it. Then I couldn't stop. It was very moreish."

Cries of approval interspersed with shouts of "Give him the money!" began rising from the audience.

Sir Percival turned to

Martin Goodbody QC for advice.

"That bear has a very valid point of law, I fear," said Mr. Goodbody. "But that doesn't alter the fact that he has to submit something to the jury for tasting. It stands to reason. I suggest failure to do that renders his entry null and void."

Paddington thought for a moment, then after another brief struggle with his hat he managed to raise it. "Here's something I made earlier," he said.

"What on earth is it?" asked Sir Percival. He gave the shapeless mound on Paddington's head a poke with his pencil. "Can't say I've come across anything like it before." He turned to the audience. "Is there a doctor in the house?"

"It's a marmalade sandwich," said Paddington.

"A marmalade sandwich?" repeated Sir Percival. "What's it doin' on top of your head?" He turned to Martin Goodbody. "How about the 'no smuggling in of other ingredients' rule?"

"Smuggling!" exclaimed Paddington hotly. He gave Sir Percival Rushmoor a hard stare. "I'm not a smuggler. I always keep one there in case I have an emergency. I'm afraid I banged my head when I was getting inside your car on the way here and it got squashed. It's very low, you know!"

"I think that answers your question, Sir Percival," said Mr. Goodbody.

Ignoring a further outburst of shouts from the audience, the judges went into a huddle.

"Perhaps we could fall back on the beef stew from number three's entry?" suggested Anne Gellica.

"I wouldn't mind falling back on a beef stew," exclaimed Paddington. "Especially if it's got dumplings in it. If they are anything like Mrs. Bird's they would be lovely and soft."

"Hold on a moment," said Sir Percival. Having licked the end of his pencil he reached for a spoon. "The proof of a good dish lies in the eating, and if this is the remains of a marmalade sandwich it tastes exceptionally good. I don't think we need look any further. I suggest you all have a go."

Paddington stood his ground while the other judges began delving in before taking it in turns to air their views.

"Heavenly!" said Anne Gellica. "Worth a star or two."

"Delish!" agreed Romney Marsh.

"Couldn't be better," announced Martin Goodbody.

"Fair dinkum," said Ron Keeps. "Wouldn't mind taking some back to the old country next time I go."

"I made it myself," said Paddington proudly. "I used some of Mrs. Bird's best marmalade. It was the 2014's. That was a very good year."

"I wouldn't mind taking her back to Australia as well," said Ron Keeps.

Back at Number thirty-two Windsor Gardens Mrs. Bird went a becoming shade of pink. "Paddington did lend a paw," she said.

Meanwhile, Paddington was addressing his gathering of admirers. "The secret is in the chunks," he explained. "I make sure there is an equal number of thick and thin ones, so there is something to please everyone. And they all point towards Darkest Peru."

"So speaks the voice of experience," said Sir Percival. "I think that says it all," he added amid general agreement as he handed Paddington an envelope.

"Don't spend it all at once," he advised.

Paddington nearly fell over backwards with surprise when he saw how much he had won.

"I shan't spend it on myself," he said. "First of all I would like to buy something nice for all the Browns for taking me in when they did, and then I would like to give the rest to the Home for Retired Bears in Lima. I'm sure they could do with it."

At which point another trumpet fanfare signaled the end of the program, and as the studio audience rose to their feet and applauded, Mrs. Bird voiced the thoughts of all those at Number thirty-two Windsor Gardens.

"I do like happy endings," she said, "and those that leave you with a taste of marmalade in the mouth are the nicest ones of all."

Chapter Six

A VISIT TO THE CLEANERS

Whether or not Mrs. Bird was right or wrong about their next-door neighbor (and it would have been most unlike her to be wrong), despite their sharing in the prize for the Best Spring Garden, it was Mr. Curry's display that drew the most attention and rubbed fresh salt into the wound every time he was seen chatting to an admirer.

People stopped to take pictures of it on their mobiles as they went past on their way to work, and again on their way home. Others with children stopped by during the day, and one or two even asked Mr. Curry for his autograph. The crowning insult of all was when a passerby said to Mr. Brown, "I bet you'd like a garden like the one next door."

There was only one way to cope with the situation and that was to grin and bear it. In any case it was spring-cleaning time at Number thirty-two Windsor Gardens and with Jonathan and Judy home for the half-term break, it was a case of all hands to the grindstone. That being so, Paddington offered to take a load of clothes to the dry cleaners in his shopping basket on wheels, and one way and another, with the help of Mrs. Brown and Mrs. Bird, in no time at all it was full almost to the brim.

"There are times when I really don't know

what we would do without a bear in the house," said Mrs. Bird, as she bustled into the kitchen after saying good-bye to him and set to work on her saucepans. "He's always so anxious to be of help."

"I bet he wouldn't be half as keen if he was a grizzly bear," said Jonathan.

Judy gave a groan. "Just for that, you can help me polish the silver," she said.

"I would if I could," replied Jonathan airily. "But I promised Dad I would have a go at his lawn mower. The blades need adjusting and it isn't a job for girls."

Mrs. Bird pointedly gave vent to a loud sigh.

To be honest, when she waved good-bye to Paddington at the front door she felt a nagging worry as to whether or not she was doing the right thing in letting him go off by himself, but she took comfort in the fact that he was a resourceful bear, and if he had a problem he could always call on Mr. Gruber for help on the way.

No doubt he would be stopping off at his best friend's antique shop for his elevenses anyway, so with strict instructions to unload his basket at the cleaners first, otherwise their promise of NO DELAY—BACK IN A DAY would be rendered null and void, she waved a final good-bye.

The Browns' housekeeper ran what Mr. Brown liked to call a "tight ship," meaning she seldom left anything to chance, but this happened to be one of those occasions when she did. Had she waited a little longer at the front door to see Paddington safely on his way, her eagle eyes would undoubtedly have spotted their next-door neighbor lingering near his front gate; but Paddington was having trouble with his steering, and it wasn't until he reached the pavement that he heard a familiar voice calling his name.

"And where might you be going, young bear?" asked Mr. Curry.

"I'm doing what Mrs. Bird calls 'The early bird catches the worm,'" said Paddington. "I'm taking some clothes to Samuels the cleaners. Mr. Samuel is expecting me."

Mr. Curry rubbed his hands in invisible soap, as was his habit when he was about to ask a favor. "I thought as much," he said. "Dear lady. She does it around this time every year. You could set your clock by it. I was hoping to catch her, but if you are going to the dry cleaners, then you are in a position to do me a small favor."

Reaching down he picked up an old carrier bag bulging at the seams. "It's all to do with my winning the prize for the Best Spring Garden in the area. One of the big dailies has got to hear of it and they are sending their top photographer to take a picture of me tending it after dark. I shall need my best suit cleaned for the occasion, and I know you won't mind adding it to your pile of old clothes. I shall make sure you are handsomely rewarded. I want to look my best in the picture, so it's a case of no expense spared."

And before Paddington had the chance to

open his mouth, Mr. Curry had placed the carrier bag on top of an already overladen basket on wheels and disappeared into his house, without so much as a "thank you."

Alarmed by the fact that the delay might make him late for the dry cleaners, Paddington did the journey in record time. To his relief, Mr. Samuel was ready and waiting when he arrived, and he helped unload the contents of the basket on wheels onto his counter.

There was a strong smell of mothballs coming from Mr. Curry's bag, and when Mr. Samuel removed the suit an actual moth flew out. "If you want my opinion," he said, "he's only just put those mothballs in. Keep an eye out for more. It's bad for business."

The suit was on a wire hanger and he held it up to the light. "As for this," he said dubiously, "it's a long time since I saw anything like it. Look at the shape of the collar for a start. If you ask me it will fall to pieces with shock if I start cleaning it."

"It belongs to our neighbor, Mr. Curry," said Paddington. "And he needs it for a special function after it gets dark."

"That's something," said Mr. Samuel. "I wouldn't fancy seeing it in daylight. On the other hand, you get to see all sorts of unexpected things in this business."

Reaching further along the counter he picked up a pair of blue jeans and held them up for Paddington to see.

"Take these," he said, pointing out several holes. "It's what's known as being distressed."

Paddington gave them a hard stare. "I'm not surprised," he said, "I'd be very distressed if I had a pair of trousers like that."

"That's as may be," said Mr. Samuel. "But you'd be surprised how many people take the opposite view. They treat it as a work of art. I know a good many who would pay through the nose to get their hands on a pair like these. The more holes there are the better—especially in the knee department. Which doesn't make our job any easier. You try cleaning something that's full of holes to start with."

"How do you make a hole in a pair of jeans?" asked Paddington.

"It's not as easy as it might sound," said Mr. Samuel. "Denim stands up to a lot of rough treatment. Sandblasting is very popular. But any way you like, provided it ends up looking like fair wear and tear and hasn't been cut out with a pair of scissors. Don't tell me you want to have a go at doing it."

"Bears don't wear jeans," said Paddington, avoiding a straight answer. "And even if I did I don't think I would want a pair looking like those."

He didn't wish to be rude, but there were times when it was hard to understand the way some humans behaved.

"It is a form of protest about life in general, with all its rules and regulations," said Mr. Samuel. "Or in some cases it's a perverted form of jealousy. A way of pointing out the difference between the 'haves' and the 'have-nots.' Saying in effect, 'It's all very well for you showing off your wealth. Just look at me— dressed in rags!'"

Looking out of his shop to make sure the coast was clear, he lowered his voice. "'No names, no pack drill,' as they used to say in the army. But some of my customers have a next-door neighbor who is very like that."

"You mean Mr. Curry?" said Paddington.

"If the cap fits," said Mr. Samuel. "I have heard tell about what happened in the front-garden competition. These things get around. Bad news travels fast, but business is business. Tell him I'll have his suit ready to be picked up by four o'clock this afternoon."

And without further ado, he brought the conversation to a close as he called for an assistant and began making a list of the various other items Paddington had delivered.

Paddington's next port of call was the bakers in the Portobello Road where he had a standing order for buns, and then a few doors down the road to the antique shop where Mr.

Gruber promptly set to work making the cocoa for their elevenses. As he did so he listened carefully to Paddington's outpourings on the subject of men's clothing and Mr. Curry.

"I only hope his suit turns up trumps," he said. "I hate to say it, but following the principle of treating others as you would wish to be treated yourself, I suggest you collect it for

him on the dot, and if you make sure it's gift-wrapped you might earn some Brownie points into the bargain."

Having thanked Mr. Gruber, Paddington hurried back to Windsor Gardens in order to lend a paw with the spring-cleaning, and it was while he was helping Jonathan adjust the lawn mower in the miniature workshop attached to the garage that he had one of his inspirations; and, as luck would have it, Mr. Brown was scrupulously neat with his tools, and there, clipped to the wall in front of him were all those needed for what he had in mind—updating the holes in Mr. Curry's suit.

It was really a case of following Mr. Gruber's advice and doing unto others what you would have them do to you, and it involved him in a certain amount of traveling to and fro, not to mention the time spent in Mr. Brown's workshop, so that it was dark by the time he had finished work.

Paddington left the parcel on Mr. Curry's doorstep, pressed the doorbell, and then made for home as fast as his legs would carry him.

The subject was never mentioned again, but the newspaper man must have turned up later that night and got what he wanted, for a full-page picture appeared in the garden section of their weekly magazine under the title HOW TO MAKE YOUR OWN FAMILY SCARE-CROW. Fortunately the designer remained uncredited.

A Visit to the Cleaners

Soon afterwards Mr. Curry was to be seen dismantling his front garden. The most ignominious moment came when he filled a wheelbarrow full of plants and, watched over by a robin redbreast, delivered them back to their rightful home.

Chapter Seven

PADDINGTON'S
FINEST HOUR

"What's a contortionist?" asked Paddington, glancing through a theater program Judy was looking at. "I don't think I have ever met one of those before. We didn't have any when I was small, and I didn't come across one in the Home for Retired Bears."

"I'm not surprised," said Jonathan. "A contortionist is someone who gets himself or herself into a funny position to entertain others. I don't suppose there are many theaters in Darkest Peru, and if you'd had one in the Home for Retired Bears it would probably have meant he was stuck like it for good."

"The one on tonight's bill is called 'Corkscrew Charlie,'" said Judy.

"I once saw him on a Royal Command Variety Performance," said Jonathan. "Even the Queen looked impressed when he unwound himself in order to take a bow."

Paddington considered the matter for a moment or two. Sometimes the things human beings did for pleasure seemed very strange to his way of thinking. "It seems a long way to come just to see someone turn himself into a corkscrew," he said. "You would have thought it would be easier for him to come to Windsor Gardens."

"I know exactly how you feel, Paddington,"

said Mr. Brown, leading them at a fast pace along a softly lit corridor. "But we haven't come all this way just to see Corkscrew Charlie. There are lots of other acts besides him, and they couldn't all come to us at once. That's why it's called a Variety Show. They were very popular when I was a boy."

"There's Fred and Mabel with their performing Pekinese dogs," said Judy, pointing to a picture on the wall. "All twelve of them."

"A laugh a minute!" broke in Jonathan, quoting from his program.

"It sounds very good value," admitted Paddington.

"And there's a team of chimpanzees doing a bicycle act," said Judy. "Fifteen of them form a giant pyramid on the handlebars of one bicycle! I bet you've never seen anything like that before either. But they don't appear until somewhere near the end of the show."

"There's something for everyone," said Mr. Brown. "Nonstop. Just like it must have been in the old days when practically every town in England had its own music hall, and entertainers similar to the ones we've been talking about were able to travel the country doing the same act all their life.

"Nowadays, one appearance on television and that's it—finished with. Millions of people have seen it and they have to find something new."

Rounding a corner they met up with a group of other latecomers being held at bay by an usherette selling programs outside a narrow doorway, and he slowed down to draw breath.

"Are you sure we're doing the right thing, Henry?" whispered Mrs. Brown. "It's rather a lot for a small bear to take in at one go. I can't help remembering the day he came to live with us and he came across a bathroom for the first time in his life. Think what a disaster that was."

Paddington looked at the others inquiringly. "Jonathan and I turned the water on and left you to it," said Judy.

"Mistake number one," said Jonathan. "You were so busy trying to write your name on the steamed-up window you forgot to turn it off and it ran over the side of the bath."

"The first we got to know about it was when water started dripping on our heads downstairs," said Mrs. Brown. "It's a wonder the whole ceiling didn't come down."

"Oh, dear," said Paddington. "But it wasn't the first bath I had ever seen. They had one in the Home for Retired Bears. It was on the roof. You should have seen the queue outside on a Friday evening. It went all round the block. So I gave up in the end. Besides, they never changed the water and Aunt Lucy said it wasn't good for a young bear. It had gone a funny color and didn't smell very nice."

"I hope he hasn't brought any 'you know whats' under his hat," whispered Judy, hastily changing the subject as the queue ahead of them noticeably edged away. "We don't want a repeat of the last time we took him to a theater. If you remember, he dropped a marmalade sandwich on a man's head in the stalls during the interval."

"Shall we *ever* forget?" said Mrs. Brown.

"I doubt very much if the man it landed on will either," broke in Mrs. Bird. "He's probably still frightened to go out after dark without a hat."

"There's no fear of that happening again," said Mr. Brown. "We were all high up in a box then alongside the upper circle and accidents happen even in the best-regulated theaters."

"I don't remember Dad saying that at the time," whispered Jonathan.

The Browns were in a part of London they had never visited before, and it had been touch-and-go as to whether or not they would make the theater in time. The last hundred yards or so after Mr. Brown had found somewhere to park the car had been frantic.

Jonathan looked up from his program.

"There's a parrot called Percy who has a spot all to himself," he said. "He walks along a tightrope blindfolded while he recites 'The boy stood on the burning deck' followed by 'To be or not to be.' In the old days he probably flew on to his next engagement."

"Nowadays he has to do a matinee every Wednesday and Saturday," added Judy. "I expect it's to make ends meet. There's a note at the bottom of the program saying someone from the RSPCA is present at all times."

"That certainly didn't happen in my day," said Mr. Brown. "It's good to hear."

121

Beyond the front of the queue there was a cacophony of sound as trumpets and trombones competed with cornets and saxophones, punctuated by an occasional burst of frantic drumming.

"That's the orchestra tuning up," explained Judy.

"I hope they get it right by the time we're inside," said Paddington.

A titter came from several people ahead of them.

"They will," said Judy. "Just you wait and see."

Paddington took a closer look at some of the pictures on the wall. "I think I might get a program while we're waiting," he announced. "It sounds very good value." And before the others had a chance to stop him, he had disappeared into the queue ahead of them.

"Oh, dear," said Mr. Brown. "I was hoping three would be enough to go round. I'm afraid he's going to be in for a shock. They don't come cheap these days."

"I strongly suspect we've encountered it already," said Mrs. Bird as she detected the sound of raised voices. "There's a bit of a commotion going on."

"It seems they've only got the souvenir programs left," said a man next to her. "And they're eight pounds fifty. We've reached a bit of an impasse. The young bear gentleman wants a receipt for his money and the girl won't give him one."

Mr. Brown heaved a sigh as he reached for his wallet. "In for a penny," he said. "In for a pound."

"He don't half have a hard stare when he likes," said the usherette when he rescued Paddington. "Never seen anything like it before."

"He only uses it when the occasion merits it," said Mr. Brown pointedly.

"The great thing about a variety show like

this," he continued as the crowd ahead of them began to move forward, "is you need to be as close to the action as possible, so I've reserved six seats in the center of Row A in the stalls."

"Is that wise, Henry?" said Mrs. Brown. "You know what Paddington's like. All it needs is a magician inviting a member of the audience onto the stage and he'll be up there like a shot—even if the man does happen to be sawing someone in half."

"*Especially* if he's sawing someone in half," murmured Jonathan as they hastily took their seats.

"There isn't a magician on the program," said Mr. Brown. "I made sure of that when I was doing the booking."

"Fingers crossed," said Judy. "At least we've got the orchestra between us and the stage. *And* we've made it in the nick of time, thank goodness!"

"Optimist," whispered Jonathan, as everything around them went quiet. "The night isn't over yet!"

The words had hardly left his mouth when a man in evening dress appeared from somewhere below the stage and climbed onto a rostrum just in front of them.

Paddington was most excited. "I could reach out and touch him," he said. "He might like one of my sandwiches. They were fresh this morning."

"I'd rather you didn't, dear," called Mrs. Brown.

The man didn't actually voice his agreement, but having bowed briefly to the audience, he turned his back on them, produced a baton from somewhere close at hand, raised it to shoulder height, and the auditorium suddenly echoed and reechoed to a brisk selection of foot-tapping tunes.

Then, as the medley came to an end, the house lights were lowered, illuminated signs on both sides of the proscenium arch showed a large figure 1, the main curtain was raised, and a troupe of Chinese acrobats swarmed onto the stage.

The Browns heaved a combined sigh of relief as they settled back in their seats and prepared to enjoy themselves.

"I'm glad the band were all in tune, Mr. Brown," called Paddington, trying to make himself heard above all the noise.

"Shh," replied Mr. Brown, trying to make himself as small as possible in the semi-darkness.

The applause at the end of what had been a boisterous first act, with hoops and dumbbells borne on waves of Oriental whoops threatening at times to drown the orchestra, was heartfelt.

Paddington's claps were as loud as anyone's when a figure 2 appeared on both sides of the stage heralding the arrival of a ventriloquist and his dummy on a unicycle.

"This is something else we didn't have in Darkest Peru, Mr. Brown," he announced excitedly.

"Bicycles are making a comeback these days," said Mr. Brown. "You haven't seen anything yet . . ."

He had certainly been correct when he stressed the fact that the show was nonstop. The theater they were in might have lacked the luxury of many in the West End of London, but as act after act followed on seamlessly, one after another, scene changes, presentation, lighting, sound couldn't be faulted.

Paddington singled out Corkscrew Charlie's act for particular praise. "I might try making some of the shapes in front of the bathroom mirror when we get back to Windsor Gardens," he announced, much to the Browns' alarm.

"Don't forget what I said," warned Judy. "You need to be careful you don't get stuck like it."

But she needn't have worried, for even as she spoke a small group of scene shifters in white overalls wheeled what looked like a large upright piano onto the stage, and in no time at all Paddington changed his mind and settled on learning to play the xylophone.

And when that act was followed by a man who had perfected the art of sending a set of white china dinner plates spinning on the end of a row of vertical walking sticks, all at the same time, it was Mrs. Bird's turn to show signs of alarm.

Having said that, apart from making a mental note to keep a watch on their china when they got back home, she had to admit the time to worry would come if Paddington eventually settled on some new fancy that lasted for more than ten minutes. As she wisely said later that evening: "He couldn't learn to do most of those things in a month of Sundays, and there was no harm in humoring him. It had to stop somewhere."

To all intents and purposes that moment came with the arrival at long last of the chimpanzees and, good though they were, Paddington wasn't sorry when they went away again. Fifteen of them perched on the handlebars of one small bicycle was wonderful in its way, but as they headed downstage at the end of their act he closed his eyes. As far as he could make out no one was actually at the controls and it felt as though they were heading straight for him.

Much to his relief, when he opened his eyes they had been replaced by a hypnotist called Kurminski the Great, who was not only the Star of the Show, but according to the program, the audience was lucky to see him at all because he was on a world tour prior to his final retirement.

"I seem to remember seeing a picture of him on a hoarding about twenty years ago," whispered Mr. Brown. "He was plain Igor Kurminski in those days and he was about to retire even then. He's put on a lot of weight since."

"Careful, Henry," hissed Mrs. Brown. "If he hears you say that he may put the 'fluence on you, and you'll be sorry."

But Mr. Kurminski's gaze was already directed to a point way above their heads.

Following a short demonstration, he commanded all those seated in the upper circle to place both hands on top of their heads, one palm over another, following which he regaled them with what was clearly his stock patter.

Mr. Brown seized the moment. "It's all part of a hypnotist's act," he said knowledgeably. "There are two things to be said about them.

"Number one is that they can't make people do things they would never, ever do of their own free will, so there is no need to worry on that score. That's an old wives' tale.

"Number two is if you get a large group of people and persuade them to clasp their hands on top of their head and leave them in that position for a while, as Kurminski the Great has just done, there are always a few who can't take them apart without help . . .

"I'm willing to bet that even now he has some assistants up there coming to the rescue of those who can't part them. All it needs is a quick snap of a finger and thumb in front of their eyes."

Turning round in their seats, a brief upward glance confirmed the truth of at least the second half of Mr. Brown's rundown on the subject.

"Did *you* ever get caught out, Dad?" called Jonathan.

But for better or worse Mr. Brown's answer was lost as the orchestra struck up a spirited rendering of the "Post Horn Gallop" to cover the confusion which reigned while order was being restored.

Meanwhile, the stage lighting was lowered, leaving the Star Turn bathed in a shaft of light from a single spotlight shining down from the back of the auditorium. The effect was eerie to say the least, and it would have been safe to say that most of those in the first few rows of the theater were doing their best not to attract Mr. Kurminski the Great's attention as he cast his eyes along the front row.

In their turn, the occupants of Row A found the word "Great" admirably suited to the person surveying them, for he seemed to tower over them like a veritable Goliath.

The comparison was Jonathan's. Apart from fanciful pictures of the Colossus of Rhodes, which in times long past once guarded the entrance to its harbor until it was destroyed by an earthquake, there was no other word for it.

Mr. Brown voiced the thoughts of the other members of the family when he said at least they were getting value for money at Jonathan's school. Whether or not the previous whispered comments had been overheard was hard to say, but from that moment the Star Turn directed his attention to the middle section of the stalls and there was a gleam in his eyes. Worse still, far from fastening his gaze on the head of the household, he was clearly concentrating on a small figure to Mr. Brown's right.

"That's torn it," groaned Jonathan.

"I knew it was too good to be true," said Judy. There was no escaping the fact that

Paddington was the chosen victim, for another smaller spotlight came into play and at a signal from Kurminski, two girl assistants emerged from the wings and bridged the orchestra pit with a small gangplank.

It was all carried out smoothly and with such precision it was over before any of the Browns had a chance to talk Paddington out of it, but he allowed himself to be escorted onto the stage with obvious pleasure.

The comparison with David and Goliath wasn't lost on others in the front row who earlier on had encountered Paddington in the queue, and the match was so blatantly unequal there was a murmur of disapproval. It only needed one to give a loud hiss before the others joined in, but Paddington remained remarkably unabashed, and a ripple of applause went round the theater as he politely raised his hat to bid Kurminski good evening.

Stifling his surprise, the Great Man felt in a waistcoat pocket and having removed a small gold watch on the end of a chain, he held it aloft and fastened his gimlet gaze on his victim.

"Look into my eyes," he said. "Then follow the path of this watch as it goes to and fro like the pendulum of a clock . . . tick tock . . . tick tock . . . tick tock."

Paddington obeyed the hypnotist's instructions as best he could, which wasn't easy because of the difference in their height, although he was much too polite to say so.

"You will find yourself falling asleep," said Kurminski the Great. "But before that happens, I want you to sing me a song."

Paddington stared at him. "Sing you a song, Mr. Minski?" he exclaimed hotly. "I'm afraid I can't do that."

"It is an order from on high," said Kurminski sternly. "It must be obeyed."

"But bears can't sing," said Paddington firmly.

"That's a first," said Jonathan. "I've never heard Paddington say bears *can't* do something before. What do you think is going to happen now?"

Looking at Paddington as though he was something the cat had brought in, the famous hypnotist went so far as to lower himself slightly, and as their eyes met again Paddington gave what must have been his hardest stare ever; twice as hard as the one he had used on the usherette was the Browns' reckoning later.

"What did you say you wanted me to do,

Mr. Minski?" he asked politely.

There was a pause of several seconds before Kurminski spoke.

"Me . . . me . . . me . . . me . . . me . . ." he gasped at long last.

Mrs. Bird leapt to her feet in the silence that followed. "Mercy me!" she cried. "Whatever next! Don't tell me he's practicing his scales."

Taking in the situation at a glance, the conductor cued a roll of drums from the percussionist and he was only just in time, for at the very same moment the key chain and watch fell to the floor with a clatter where they lay unregarded as the Great Man tossed his head back and in disappointingly cockney accents gave voice to "My Old Man's a Dustman."

There was a moment's pause and then a deafening wave of applause swept through the theater, although whether it was for Kurminski the Great's rendering of the song or for Paddington's hard stare was anybody's guess.

Clearly the orchestra was taken by surprise, for there was a flurry of music sheets, but almost at once, led by the pianist, they produced a suitable backing. For a few moments all was confusion.

The stage manager rushed on and ordered them to play something lively, so they broke into the "Tritsch Tratsch Polka," which was clearly kept for any emergency.

"It's all your fault, bear!" he barked, turning to address Paddington. "Do something!"

"Click your paws," called the conductor. "Can't you see? He's in a trance."

"I'm afraid bears can't click their paws either," said Paddington.

"Well, you shouldn't be going around hypnotizing people then," said the stage manager accusingly.

Paddington gave him another of his hard stares.

The stage manager backed away. "Go away," he said.

"It's his summer birthday," called Mrs. Bird. "Bears have two every year—like the Queen." She turned to the others. "What a shame his Aunt Lucy isn't here to witness it."

"I wouldn't mind betting she heard the applause in Darkest Peru," said Judy. "It felt loud enough."

Cries of "More! More!" came from all sides, from the stalls and from the circle until it felt as though it would never stop—then, as suddenly as it had started it came to a halt.

It was a masterstroke on the part of the stage manager. He could have had a riot on his hands. Instead of which he ordered the national anthem to be played.

One moment it had been a bedlam of noise with people thronging the aisles—the next it had disappeared as they shuffled quietly out through the open doors, leaving only the sound of ladies with dustpans and brushes and vacuum cleaners to show where they had all been.

The usherette selling the programs came rushing up. "To think," she said. "He gave *me* one of his hard stares! Can I have his autograph?"

For those who saw the parallel with David and Goliath it had undoubtedly been Paddington's Finest Hour, and soon a small queue began to form so they were the last to leave the theater.

"It's been a lovely birthday," he said, as they eventually drove out of the car park and the sound of "My Old Man's a Dustman" faded into the distance. "Bears' stares last for a long time, but they don't last forever."

"That's life, Paddington," said Mr. Brown. "One moment you're up—the next moment you're down. That applies to us all."

"I think," said Paddington, "when we get back home I wouldn't mind taking singing lessons."

"That's exactly what I meant," said Mr. Brown, amid general agreement. "One way and another it applies to us all. Someone has to suffer."

Read and Discover Paddington!